# WELCOME TO
# KEEP L.O.V.E. PRESENT
# The
# "World of WOW"

# The MIRACLE LVE COLLECTION
# FEATURING

Inspired through J.E. Jackson and N.S. Muslim

# LESSONS OF VITAL ENERGY

**Published by:**
The ML Wisebrary Collection
Email – mlcollection1@gmail.com
Website – keeplovepresent.com

KLP, Publisher
J. E. Jackson, Editorial Director
Yvonne Rose/Quality Press, Book Packager
N. S, Muslim, Cover and Text Illustrator
Printed Page, Cover & Text Formatting

ALL RIGHTS RESERVED

No part of this book may be reproduced or transmitted in any form or by any means – electronic or mechanical, including photocopying, recording or by any information storage and retrieved system without written permission from the authors, except for the inclusion of brief quotations in a review.

The publication is sold with the understanding that the Publisher is not engaged in rendering legal or other professional services. If legal advice or other expert assistance is required, the services of a competent professional person should be sought.

ML Wisebrary Books are available at special discounts for bulk purchases, sales promotions, fund raising or educational purposes.

Copyright 2015 © by Jacqueline Rozier and Naim S. Muslim
ISBN #: 978-09964951-1-0
Library of Congress Control Number: 2015944952

# W.O.W-FULLY ENTER L.O.V.E. CONVERSATIONS OF MIRACLES EVERYDAY

WELCOME TO OUR WORLD OF MIRACLE Ls
WELCOME TO OUR WORLD OF WONDERMENT WAY BIGGER THAN A WHALE

WELCOME TO OUR WORLD OF COLORFUL CELEBRATION
WELCOME TO OUR WORLD OF JUMPING JUBILATION

WELCOME TO OUR WORLD OF FUN AND JOY
WELCOME TO OUR WORLD TO EVERY GIRL AND EVERY BOY

WELCOME TO OUR WORLD OF INSPIRING THE LOVE IN YOU
WELCOME TO OUR WORLD OF ANOTHER KIND OF NEW

WELCOME TO L.O.V.E. WORDS AND NEW WAYS
WELCOME TO WONDERFUL W.O.W.-FULLY DAYS

WELCOME TO OUR WORLD OF W.O.W.!
WELCOME TO OUR WORLD OF NOW!

WELCOME TO OUR WORLD OF L.O.V.E.!
WE WELCOME YOU WITH A BUBBLING BOW!

# LESSONS

are

**L**earning
**E**veryday
**S**killfully
**S**tudying
**O**ne's
**N**ewness
**S**uccessfully

# Lessons are for ME

# Lessons come from EVERYWHERE

# To teach us how to "BE"

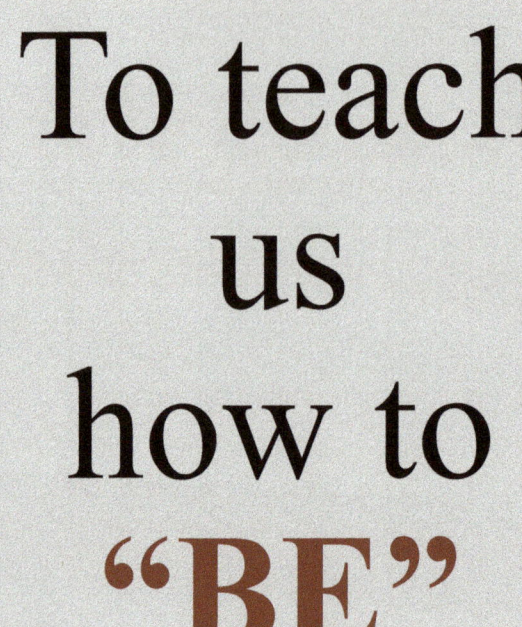

# Lessons
## prepare us for
## L.I.F.E.

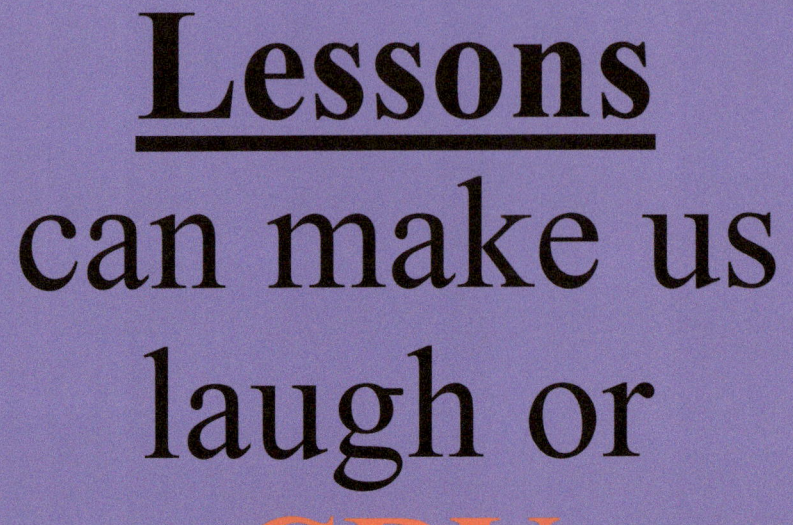

# Lessons live in the heart and the MIND

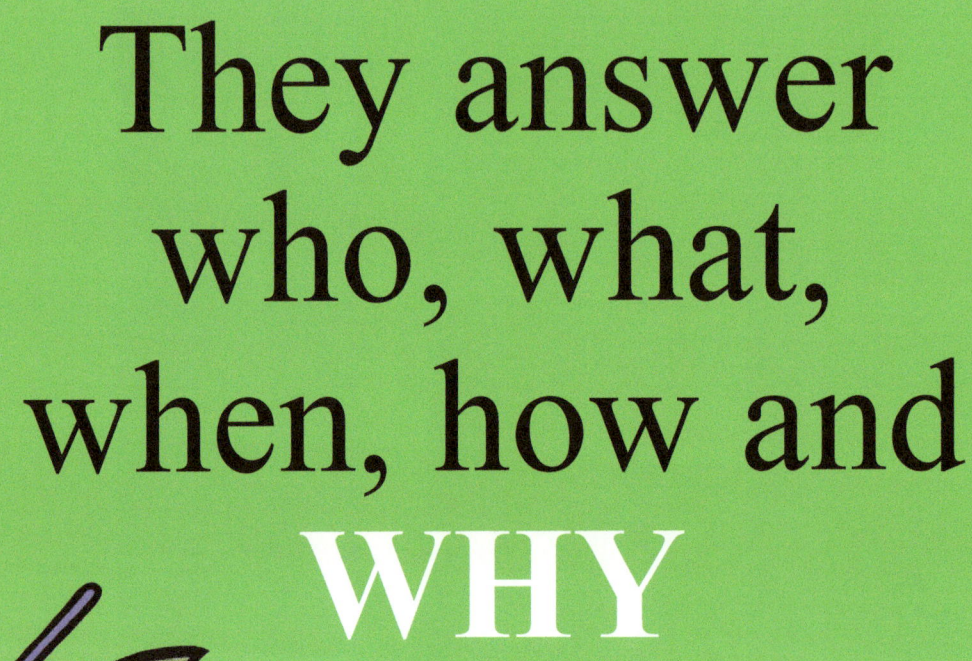

# Lessons
inspire us how to show **L.O.V.E.**

# Lessons are all AROUND

# Lessons
## are up in the sky ABOVE

# Lessons
## are deep in the GROUND

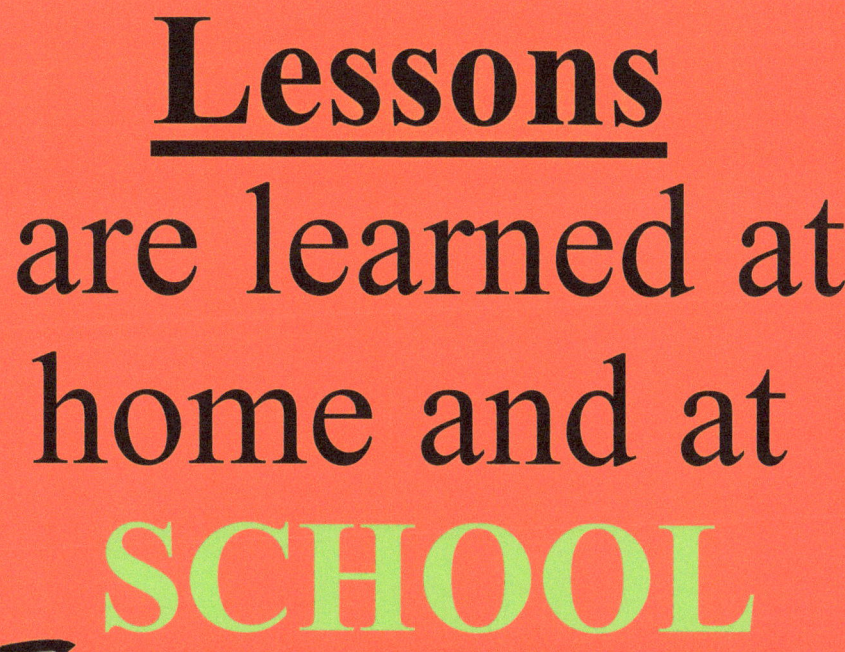

# Lessons
are learned at home and at SCHOOL

# Where we learn math, spelling and how to put on our SHOES

And how to make the color green when we mix yellow and BLUE

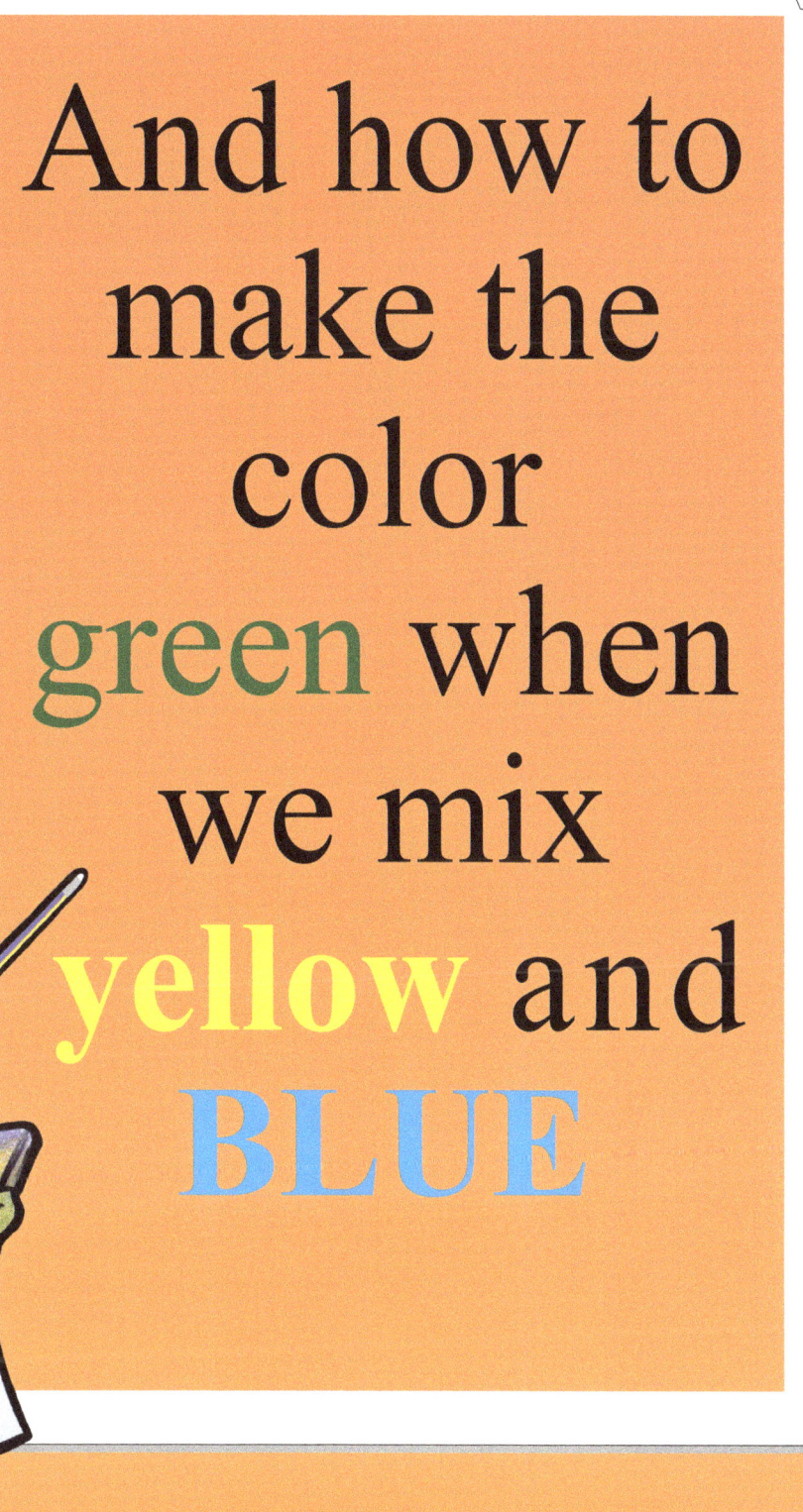

# Neighbors, parents, teachers and all the WHOMEVERS

They teach us knowledge, wisdom, and instruct us with L.O.V.E.

# It's a W.O.W.fully world where all creation learns **TOGETHER**

# When at work and when at PLAY

# Lessons
## are how everything in life is TAUGHT

# Lessons
## are learned all around the WORLD

# And create memories in every HEART

# Lessons come from fish, birds and ANIMALS

# Lessons
## come from flowers, trees and
## PLANTS

# Lessons
## come through
## CREATION

# From the large whale in the ocean and the tiny little ANT

# Lessons

can be learned from the moon and stars at **NIGHT**

# And the early morning sunrise that shines so **BRIGHT**

# Do you believe Lessons are BLESSINGS?

Lightning Source UK Ltd.
Milton Keynes UK
UKHW050455090920
369560UK00007B/111